D0121440

I cannot wait for you to see

how **great** the world can be . . .

. . . and it will be more wonderful

with you alongside me.

I cannot wait to **teach** you
how to do the things I do.

I'll share and show all that I know
and **learn** new things from you.

Side by side,

we'll walk the world.

We'll make a super team!

And troubles shared are **never** quite as bad as they first seem.

And one day not so far from now,

you'll walk ahead of me.

I'll watch your steps with happiness.
I know how **proud** I'll be.

And even when you're quite grown-up
and life's in front of you . . .

. . . what I'll **wish** for most . . .

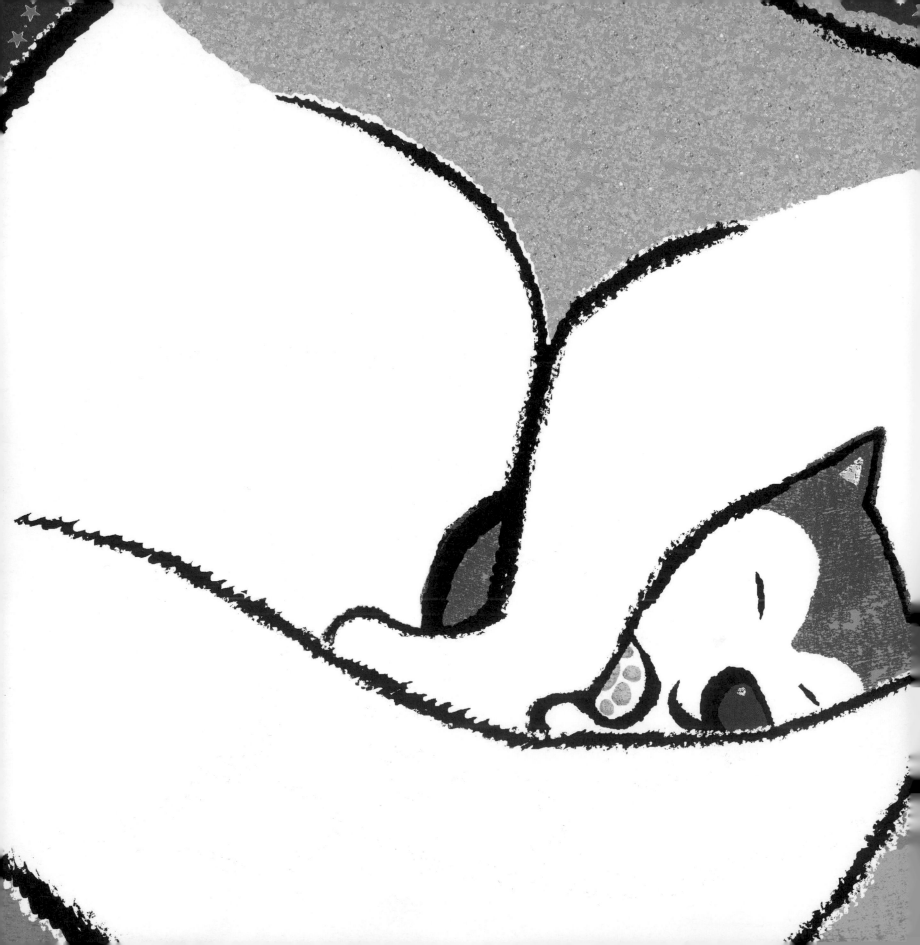

. . . is that your **wishes** all come **true.**

First published 2014 by Nosy Crow Ltd
The Crow's Nest, 10a Lant Street
London SE1 1QR
www.nosycrow.com

This edition published 2016

ISBN 978 0 85763 766 6 (PB)

Nosy Crow and associated logos are trademarks
and/or registered trademarks of Nosy Crow Ltd.

Text and illustration © Emma Dodd 2014

The right of Emma Dodd to be identified as
the author and illustrator of this work has been asserted.

A CIP catalogue record for this book is available from the British Library.

Printed in China
Papers used by Nosy Crow are made from
wood grown in sustainable forests.

1 3 5 7 9 8 6 4 2 (PB)